For grieving children and families everywhere

Because The Sky Is Everywhere

Written by Nancy Sharp

Illustrated by David Dodson

Eleven Eleven Press

Because the Sky is Everywhere
Written by Nancy Sharp
Illustrated by David Dodson

© 2017 Nancy Sharp

Published by

Eleven Eleven Press

Illustrations: David Dodson, www.2dartstudio.weebly.com
Cover and Interior Layout: Nick Zelinger, www.NZGraphics.com
Text: Footlight MT Light

ISBN: 978-0-9981739-0-0 (softcover)
Library of Congress Cataloging in Publication Data on File

First Edition
Printed in the United States of America

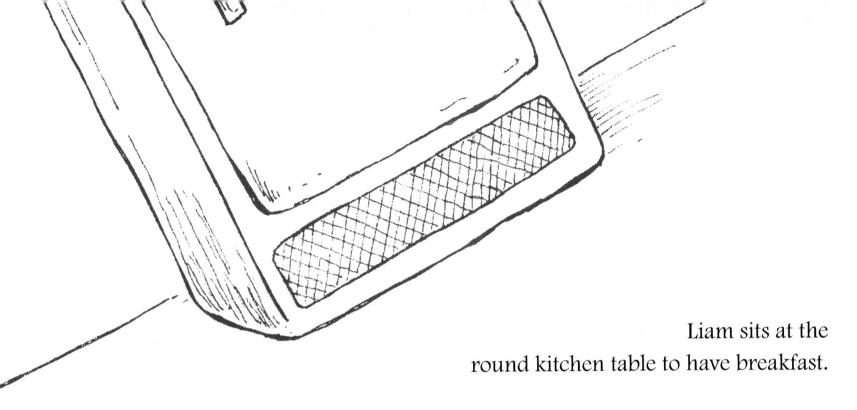

Liam sits at the
round kitchen table to have breakfast.

He eats cereal from his bowl.

Everything feels the same.

Except nothing is the same.

Liam's father died.

He must be hiding,
Liam thinks.

Liam searches behind
the fat chair in the living room.

He searches in the pantry.

He searches in Daddy's cedar closet, pushing aside the big jar of coins and shoes.

Daddy is nowhere to be found.

Maybe Daddy
went for a walk.

Maybe he's sitting
on a bench watching
the boats at the harbor.

Maybe he drove a
fancy sports car
on the highway.

Liam imagines a flock of noisy seagulls
flying overhead.

Higher and higher they go.

The seagulls give him an idea.

He dreams of the
tallest tree he can.

When he reaches
the top, he searches
for his Daddy
far and wide.

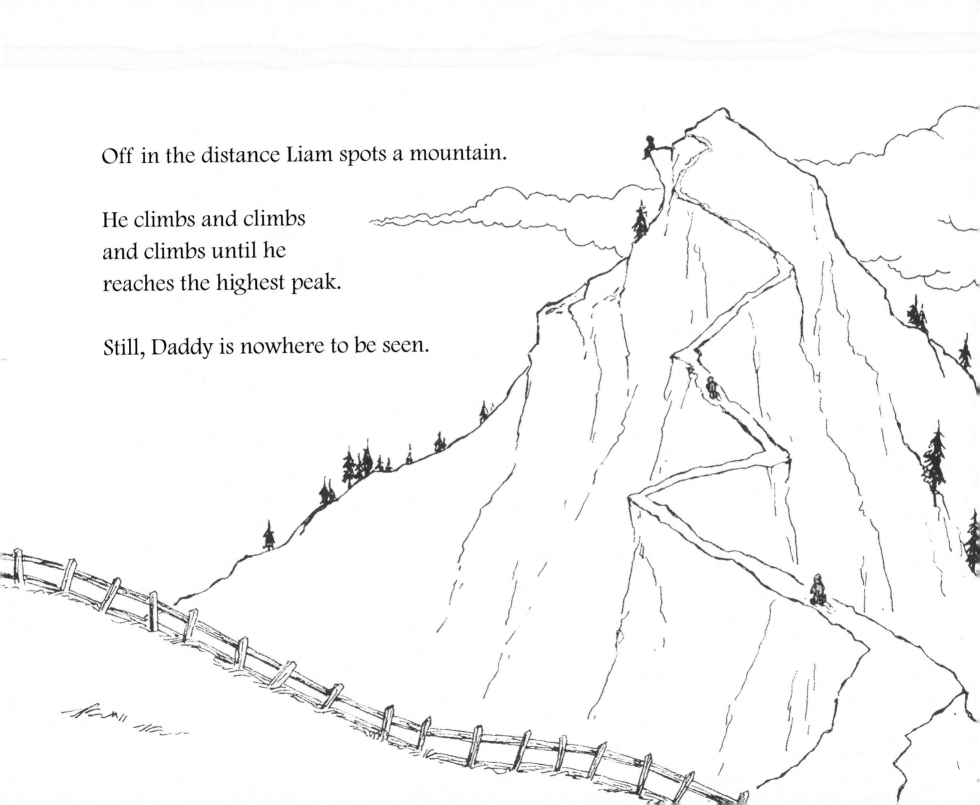

Off in the distance Liam spots a mountain.

He climbs and climbs
and climbs until he
reaches the highest peak.

Still, Daddy is nowhere to be seen.

It's dark now.

Liam lies down, small and
  a little unsure as he looks up
    at the maze of stars that dot the sky.

The stars look very far away.

Liam thinks…

Daddy must be in the sky.

He hops onto a tall cloud
that brings him straight up to the stars.

He hovers near one star.

And then another.

And another.

Until he spots what looks like Daddy's outstretched arms in the shape of a star.

And his briefcase in another.

And his golf club in another.

Liam jumps up and down because he's sure that he sees
Daddy's smile in the brightest star of all.

And there.

And there.

Daddy, it seems, is everywhere.

Liam wishes that he could stay in the sky forever.

But his mother and sister and puppy are probably missing him back home.

Just as he turns to leave, something magical happens.

The sky brightens. Liam hears an echo…

Love is everywhere   where   where   where.

Liam smiles for the first time all day and floats home.

The sky is so many things at once.

Best of all...

the sky is everywhere.

Author's Note

This book was inspired by real conversations and dreams by my twins. They were three years old. Their father had died the year before, and they struggled to understand just where he was. Death is a hard enough concept for adults to grasp, but it's all the more abstract for small children. Just like Liam, my twins searched in obvious places around our home and neighborhood before coming to believe that their daddy might be elsewhere. They came to this realization on their own in the midst of a car ride.

"Where is Daddy?" my daughter Rebecca asked.

"Daddy is in the sky," answered her brother Casey.

"Is the sky back that way Mama?"

"No," said Casey, "the sky is everywhere."

What I have tried to portray in *Because the Sky is Everywhere* is the universal longing for reassurance that children feel when someone close to them dies. While they may not have lasting memories, they still find comfort knowing that love can be felt in innumerable ways. Love is in the family photographs, in the stories told around the dinner table, in the shared activities, rituals, jokes, and in the arms of the family, friends, people, and pets who are still with them. When the physical world feels too painful to hold, they can learn to visualize a protective place or being just like Liam.

Only by loving fully can we honor those whose absences we mourn.

I am eternally grateful to my twins, who are now teenagers. Losing their father has made them more compassionate, sensitive people.

And to my second husband Steve, and stepsons Ryan and Dylan, who experienced a similar loss to ours, I have this to say: love is as infinite as the sky.

A note about the wonderful illustrations by David Dodson, whose pen and ink beautifully capture Liam's yearning and journey toward acceptance. Readers will see that in the beginning pages of the book only Liam is in color but for a sliver of blue sky. It's only when Liam gains awareness that just as the sky is everywhere, so, too, is his father's love, that his world is filled with color once again.

Both Sides Now: A True Story of Love, Loss, and Bold Living

Both Sides Now hinges on the day when Nancy Sharp delivered premature twins and learned that her husband's cancer had returned after eighteen months in remission. Set in New York City where the couple lived happily until Brett's shocking diagnosis in 1998, the story moves back in time through Nancy and her husband's courtship and marriage—and forward through Brett's death, when the twins were two and a half, he was not-quite forty, and Nancy was thirty-seven.

When life hands you the unthinkable, you must find new ways to see. Such is the ground on which Nancy rebuilt her world. She did so in Denver, Colorado after a chance conversation with a friend convinced her to take the leap of faith she needed. And so she came with her five-year-old twins, never expecting to find love again in the pages of a magazine. This is a story of real courage and unexpected joy. It is also a story about Steve, Nancy's second husband, a widower with two children, and of the surprising turns life takes when blending two families torn by loss. *Both Sides Now* promises hard-won wisdom, a gift for those looking to rise again: *The past is simply part of our story, but not the whole story.*

"Eloquent and fiercely hopeful." —***Kirkus Reviews***

"*Both Sides Now* is an unflinching memoir of love and loss and hope. Nancy Sharp's honesty and hard-earned wisdom make this book essential reading for anyone facing adversity—which is all of us."

—Ann Hood, Author of *Comfort* and *The Book That Matters Most*

"As a chaplain and grief counselor, I am asked to read many books written by grievers about their grief journey. Never before has a book made me feel as connected to the writer as Nancy Sharp's *Both Sides Now*."

—Brenda F. Atkinson, M.Div, CT, Continuing Care Coordinator, Thomas McAfee Funeral Homes
Contributor, *Grief Perspectives*

"Sharp's memoir tells of a familiar story of becoming widowed and finding a way forward, but this book stands out for its uncommon insight, wit, empathy and powerful momentum." **—Rev. Paul A. Metzler, DMin, Editor,**
Association Death Education Counseling Forum,
Books Review Editor, *Omega–Journal of Death and Dying*

About The Author

Nancy Sharp is a keynote speaker and author of the memoir *Both Sides Now: A True Story of Love, Loss, and Bold Living*, winner of eight literary honors, including Books For A Better Life and the Colorado Book Award. Her writing has been included in numerous national media and *The Best Advice in Six Words*.

As a motivational speaker, Nancy teaches audiences how to move from stuck, disappointment, and loss of all kinds toward growth and positive change. She speaks on the theme of bold living.

Nancy holds an MFA in Creative Nonfiction from Goucher College. She lives in Denver, Colorado with her husband Steve Saunders and their four children, ages fifteen through twenty-five.

www.NancySharp.net

About the Illustrator

David Dodson lives in Santa Clarita, California and has been passionate about drawing for as long as he can remember. He holds an Associate Degree in Art and has illustrated many children's books, graphic novels, and other commissioned works.

www.2dartstudio.weebly.com